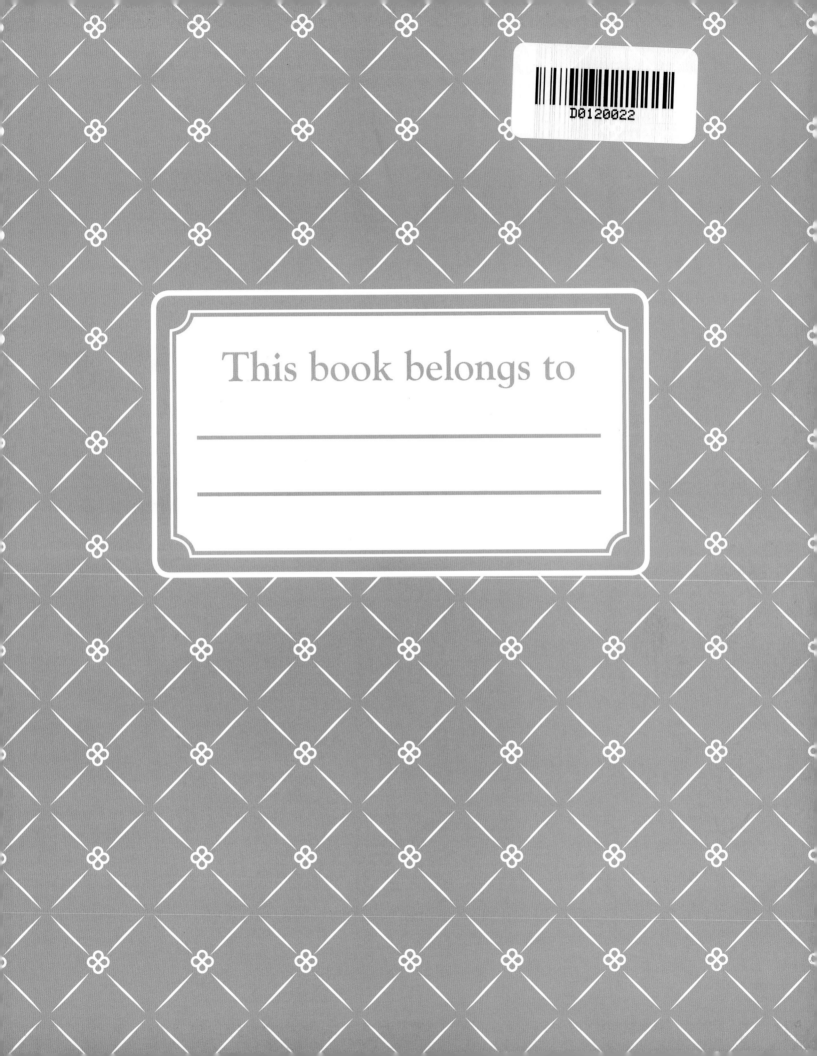

This book belongs to

This edition published by Parragon Books Ltd in 2016

Parragon Books Ltd
Chartist House
15–17 Trim Street
Bath BA1 1HA, UK
www.parragon.com

ISBN 978-1-4748-4080-4

Printed in China

Disney MOVIE COLLECTION
A SPECIAL DISNEY STORYBOOK SERIES

DUMBO

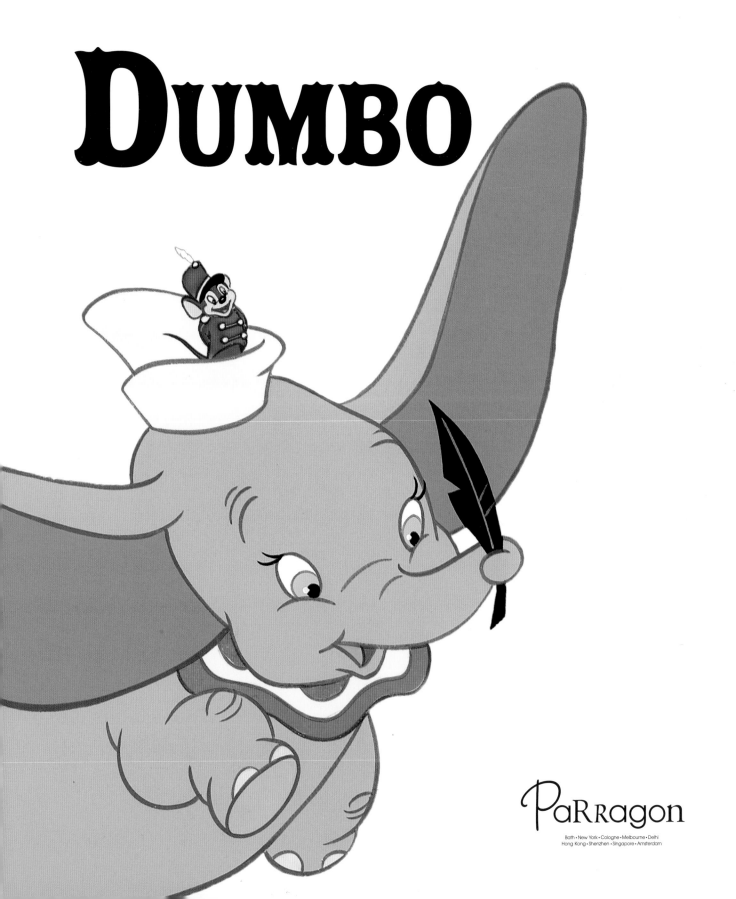

PaRragon

Bath • New York • Cologne • Melbourne • Delhi
Hong Kong • Shenzhen • Singapore • Amsterdam

Early one morning, before the stars had left the sky, a flock of storks flew high over the sleeping countryside, carrying some very special bundles. Inside the bundles were new little baby animals, waiting to be delivered to their mothers.

Far below, the lead stork saw the tents and trailers of a circus. "Release your bundles!" he shouted.

From her pen, Mrs Jumbo watched the bundles floating down. Surely one of them held her own little baby, she thought, as one parcel after another dropped gently to the ground.

One bundle held a fuzzy little bear cub. A funny baby kangaroo peeked out of another. And in another was a long-necked baby giraffe. But no special bundle came for Mrs Jumbo.

As the animals boarded the train the next morning, Mrs Jumbo did not want to leave. As she climbed into the elephant car, she searched the sky again.

Where, oh where was the bundle with her little baby?

"All aboard!" shouted the Ringmaster. "All aboard!"

Casey Junior whistled. With a powerful tug, he headed down the track. Once again the circus was on its way.

Mr Stork flew down to the little train and landed on the roof of a train carriage. "Oh, Mrs Jumbo! Special delivery for Mrs Jumbo!" he called, hopping from one train carriage to the next.

From one carriage, Mr Stork saw several elephant trunks waving at him. "Yoo-hoo! Yoo-hoo! In here! In here!" the elephants called.

Mr Stork hopped into the train carriage. "Which one of you ladies is
expecting a little bundle of joy?" he asked.

"Right over there," the elephants answered, pointing to Mrs Jumbo.

She smiled shyly as Mr Stork placed the bundle at her feet, cleared his
throat and began to recite. "Here is a baby with eyes of blue, straight from
heaven – right to you!"

"Do hurry, dearie," the other elephants urged as Mrs Jumbo began to untie the bundle with her trunk.

"Oooh!" Everyone cooed when the bundle fell open. For there sat an adorable baby elephant, with a sweet little trunk and big blue eyes.

"What are you going to call him?" the elephants asked Mrs Jumbo.

"Jumbo Junior," she replied proudly.

"Kootchy, kootchy, koo!" one elephant said, tickling the baby beneath his chin.

"Aaachoo!" the little elephant sneezed. His ears, which had been neatly tucked behind his head, flopped open. They were enormous!

The elephants shrieked with laughter. "Just look at those ears," one elephant giggled. "Why, with those ears, you should call him 'Dumbo'!"

The elephants' teasing made Mrs Jumbo angry. Turning her back on the others, she picked up her baby, carried him to a corner of the train car and lay down beside him.

She didn't care if her baby's ears were big. She thought he was beautiful just the way he was. Cuddling him in her trunk, she gently rocked him to sleep.

The next day, the townspeople followed the parade to the circus ground. "Hurry, hurry, hurry! Step right up and get your tickets!" The circus barker called to the gathering crowd.

Inside the elephant tent, Mrs Jumbo was quietly bathing Dumbo when a bunch of rowdy boys ran in.

"Look at those ears!" they shouted when they saw Dumbo. "Isn't that the funniest thing you ever saw?" The boys wiggled their ears and stuck out their tongues at Dumbo.

Dumbo tried to hide behind his mother, but the boys wouldn't leave him alone. Laughing and jeering, they crawled beneath the ropes and pulled his ears.

Mrs Jumbo wanted to protect her baby. She picked up a bale of straw and threw it at the boys to scare them away.

"Help! Mad elephant!" they screamed.

The Ringmaster dashed into the tent. "Down, Mrs Jumbo!" he shouted, cracking his whip in the air.

Then someone tried to pull Dumbo away. Furious, Mrs Jumbo bellowed and charged.

"Wild elephant! Wild elephant!" the people screamed, running in all directions.

Animal trainers threw ropes around Mrs Jumbo, who fought and strained against them.

But Mrs Jumbo was no match
for the men and their strong
ropes. At last, she was too
exhausted to fight anymore.

"Lock her up," the
Ringmaster commanded.

As Dumbo watched, the
trainers dragged his mother
away. They locked her in a
carriage that was set apart
from the rest of the circus.

There, with her legs in
chains, Mrs Jumbo stood alone,
weeping for her baby.

Dumbo, crying for his mother, thought he had no friends in the world as the other elephants turned their back on him.

But Dumbo was wrong. Someone did want to be his friend. In a corner of the tent sat a little mouse named Timothy. When he saw how the other elephants treated poor Dumbo, it made him mad.

"Look at that poor little fella," the little mouse said. "Everyone's making fun of his ears. What's the matter with them? I think they're cute."

But Dumbo was scared of Timothy, at first. Timothy found him hiding beneath a pile of hay.

"Aw, you aren't afraid of little old me, are you?" Timothy asked. "I'm Timothy Mouse, and I'm your friend, Dumbo. I have a plan to help you free your mother."

At that, Dumbo forgot all about being scared. He crawled out of the hay and listened wide-eyed to everything his new friend had to say.

"I know you're embarrassed by your ears, kid," Timothy said. "But lots of people with big ears are famous. So all we gotta do is make you a big star. But first we need a really colossal act. And I'm just the fellow to think of one. Leave everything to me."

The next day, Timothy put his plan to make Dumbo a star into action.

The Ringmaster blew his whistle and the first elephant climbed on top of a large ball.

Dumbo and Timothy watched as the pyramid rose higher and higher, until it almost reached the top of the tent.

"And now, Ladies and Gentlemen," the Ringmaster shouted, "the world's smallest elephant will spring to the top of the pyramid!"

But before Dumbo could make his leap, his ears came untied and he stumbled over them, right into the elephant pyramid.

For a moment, the stunned crowd watched in silence as the elephant pyramid teetered and swayed. Then they ran for their lives as the elephants began to fall.

Trumpeting and bellowing, the elephants tumbled down, crashing into beams and platforms and audience seats. They smacked into walls and pulled down wires and ropes. Finally, they crashed into the centre tent pole.

The enormous tent began to sway and billow.
Then, with a huge groan, it collapsed. Dumbo was left
sitting alone and forlorn in the middle of the ruins.

The very next show, the clowns painted Dumbo's face and
dressed him as a baby. They put him on a tiny platform high up
in a building surrounded by crackling, make-believe flames.
Dumbo stood shaking with fear, while far below, clowns
dressed as firemen ran around squirting hoses at each other.

"The baby will have to jump!" the chief clown fireman announced. The firemen held up a thin safety net. Closing his eyes, Dumbo leaped from the building.

Dumbo fell through the net and landed in a tub of wet plaster. The audience roared with laughter. As the clowns bowed to the cheering crowds, they paid no attention to Dumbo, who crept from the tent feeling hurt, humiliated and miserable.

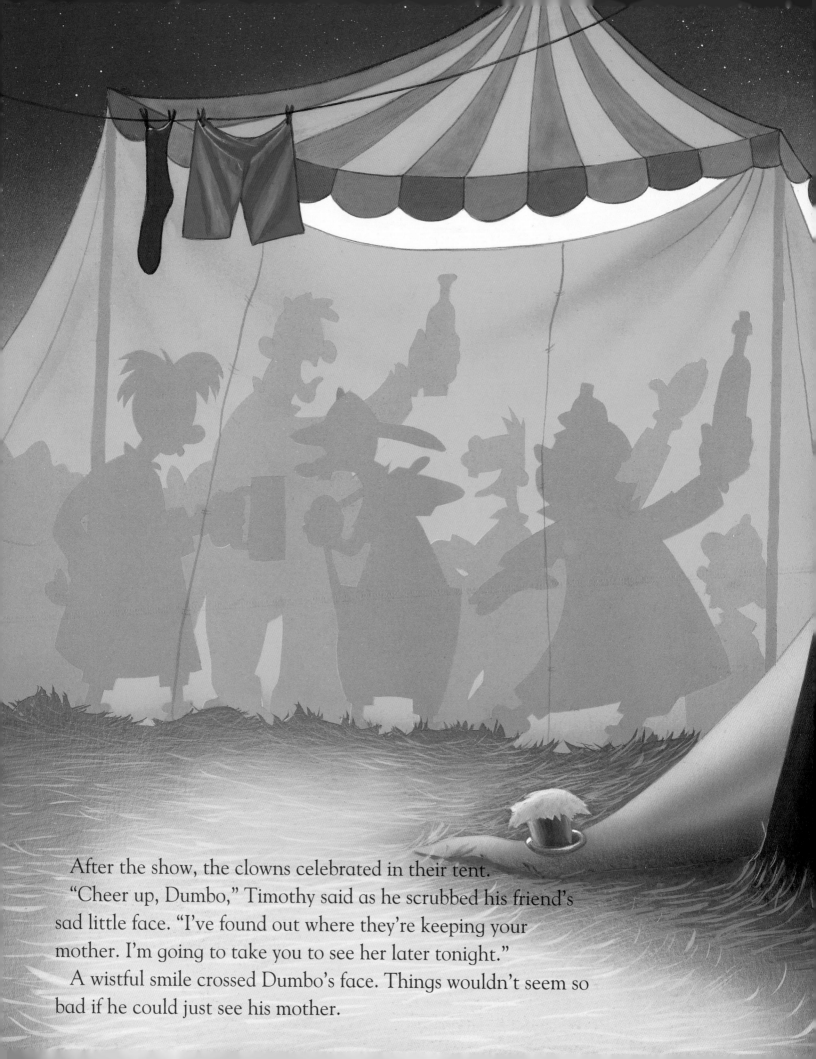

After the show, the clowns celebrated in their tent.

"Cheer up, Dumbo," Timothy said as he scrubbed his friend's sad little face. "I've found out where they're keeping your mother. I'm going to take you to see her later tonight."

A wistful smile crossed Dumbo's face. Things wouldn't seem so bad if he could just see his mother.

Later that night, while most of the circus folk slept, Timothy took
Dumbo to the carriage where his mother was chained.

"Mrs Jumbo, someone to see you!" Timothy called.

Mrs Jumbo put her trunk through the bars of the window and
stroked Dumbo's head. She wrapped her trunk around Dumbo and
rocked him lovingly.

At last it was time to leave. Tearfully, Dumbo and his mother
waved goodbye.

As Timothy and Dumbo returned to the clowns' tent, they heard the clowns talking about their act. "Let's make the house taller tomorrow," shouted a clown.

"Be careful," warned another clown. "We don't want to hurt the little guy."

"Aw, you can't hurt an elephant. They're made of rubber!" The first clown waved his hand scornfully. No one noticed that in his excitement, he knocked a bottle into Dumbo's tub.

The clown's words hurt Dumbo's feelings and he began to cry again. He sobbed so hard, he got the hiccups. "You need a nice, long drink of water," Timothy said, leading Dumbo to the tub.

Obediently, Dumbo took a big gulp. Suddenly his eyes grew heavy and his ears drooped. "Hey, what kind of water is this?" Timothy asked.

As he leaned over the tub, he fell in. When he climbed back out, Timothy had a strange look on his face. They both had some very odd dreams that night ...

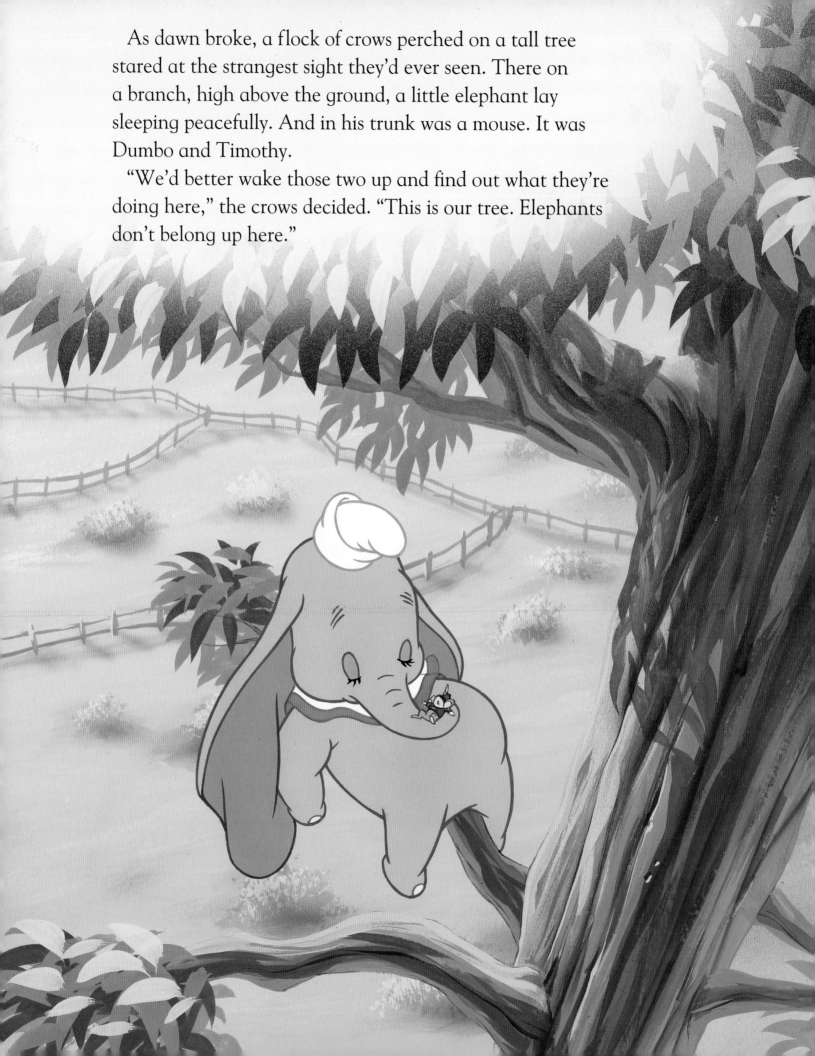

As dawn broke, a flock of crows perched on a tall tree stared at the strangest sight they'd ever seen. There on a branch, high above the ground, a little elephant lay sleeping peacefully. And in his trunk was a mouse. It was Dumbo and Timothy.

"We'd better wake those two up and find out what they're doing here," the crows decided. "This is our tree. Elephants don't belong up here."

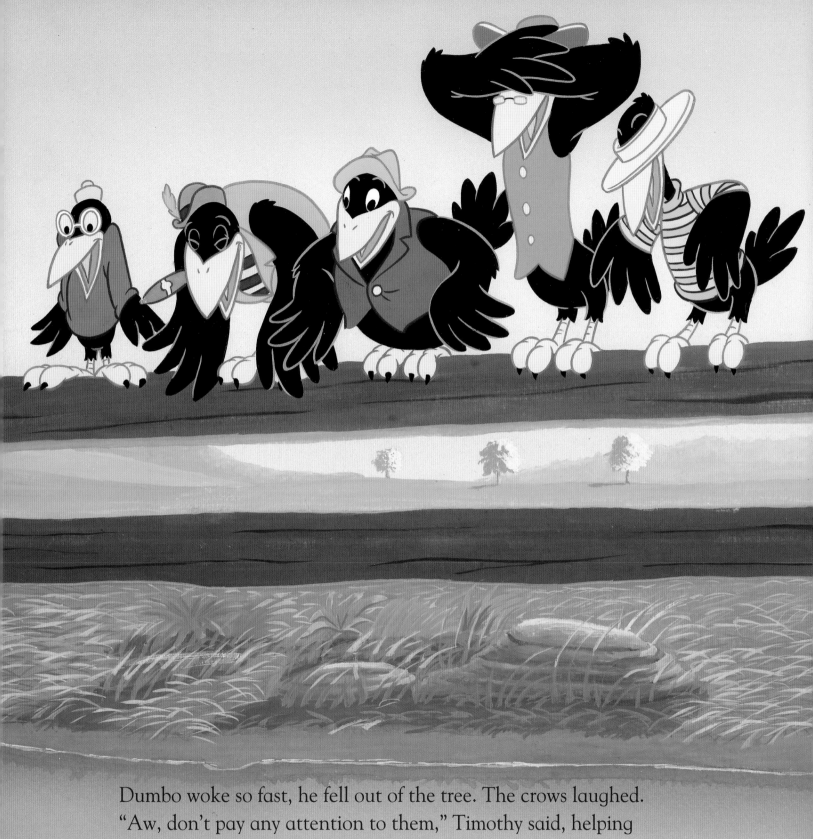

Dumbo woke so fast, he fell out of the tree. The crows laughed.

"Aw, don't pay any attention to them," Timothy said, helping
Dumbo up. "I do wonder how we got up in that tree, though."

"Maybe you flew!" one of the crows shouted.

"Oh, sure." Timothy shrugged his shoulders. "Maybe we – "
Timothy stopped and stared at Dumbo's ears. "That's it, Dumbo!" he
exclaimed. "Your ears! They're perfect wings! You're the world's only
flying elephant!"

The crows started laughing at Dumbo.

"You should be ashamed, picking on a little fella like that!" Timothy scolded them.

The crows felt bad. One of them handed Timothy a black feather. "Tell him this is a magic feather," he said, "and so long as he holds onto it, he can fly."

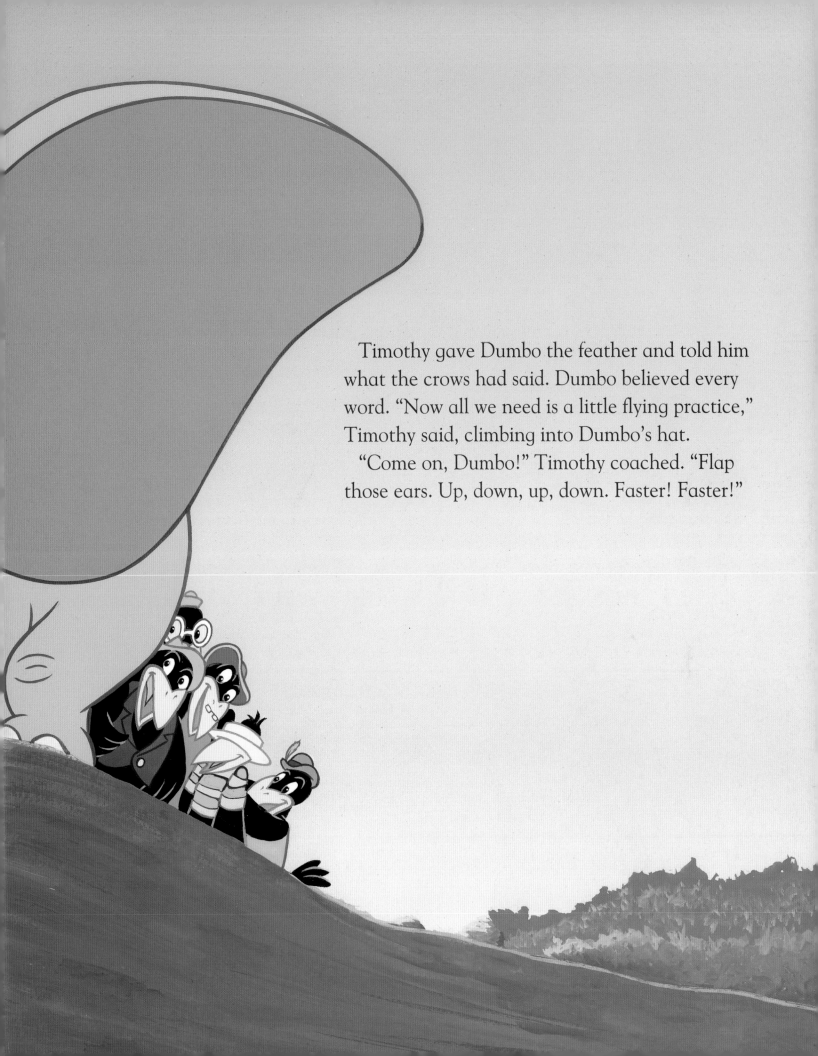

Timothy gave Dumbo the feather and told him what the crows had said. Dumbo believed every word. "Now all we need is a little flying practice," Timothy said, climbing into Dumbo's hat.

"Come on, Dumbo!" Timothy coached. "Flap those ears. Up, down, up, down. Faster! Faster!"

Dumbo clutched his feather, closed his eyes, flapped his ears, and suddenly he was soaring.

The crows flew alongside the little elephant, cheering him on. "Why, he flies just like an eagle. Better than an aeroplane!" they crowed.

"Hot diggity! You're flying! You're really flying!" Timothy shouted. "I knew you could do it! Wait till the next performance. We'll show everyone what you can do!"

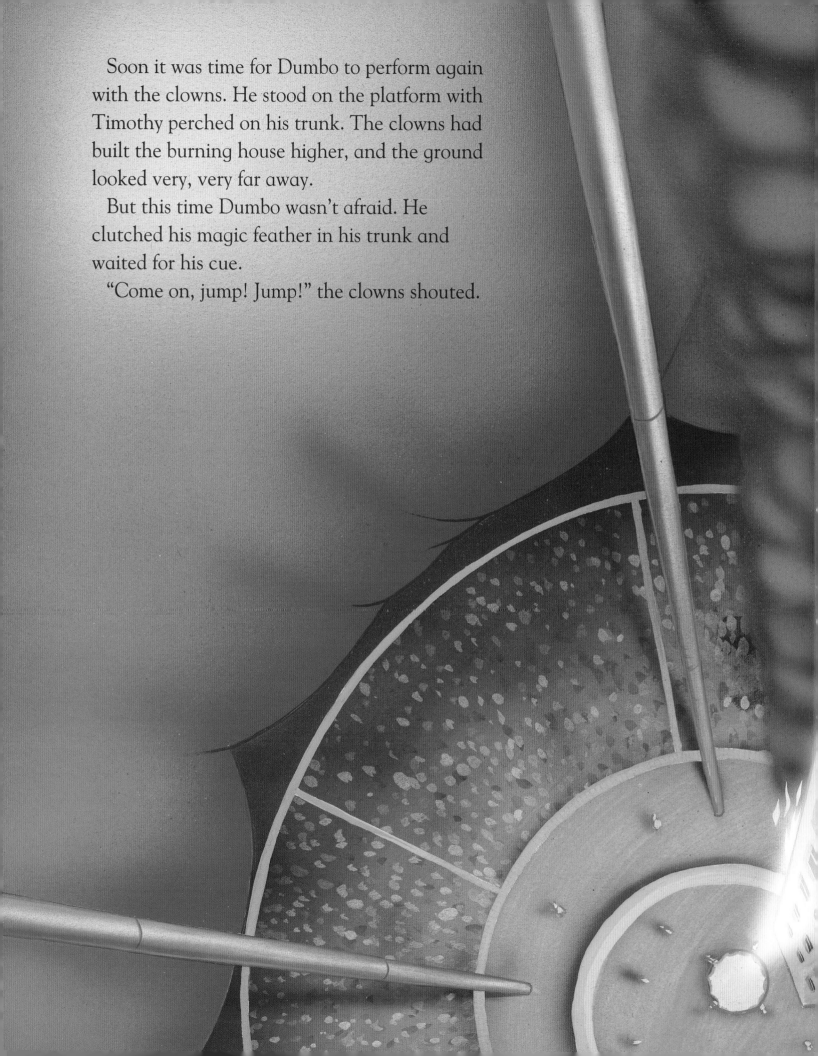

Soon it was time for Dumbo to perform again
with the clowns. He stood on the platform with
Timothy perched on his trunk. The clowns had
built the burning house higher, and the ground
looked very, very far away.

But this time Dumbo wasn't afraid. He
clutched his magic feather in his trunk and
waited for his cue.

"Come on, jump! Jump!" the clowns shouted.

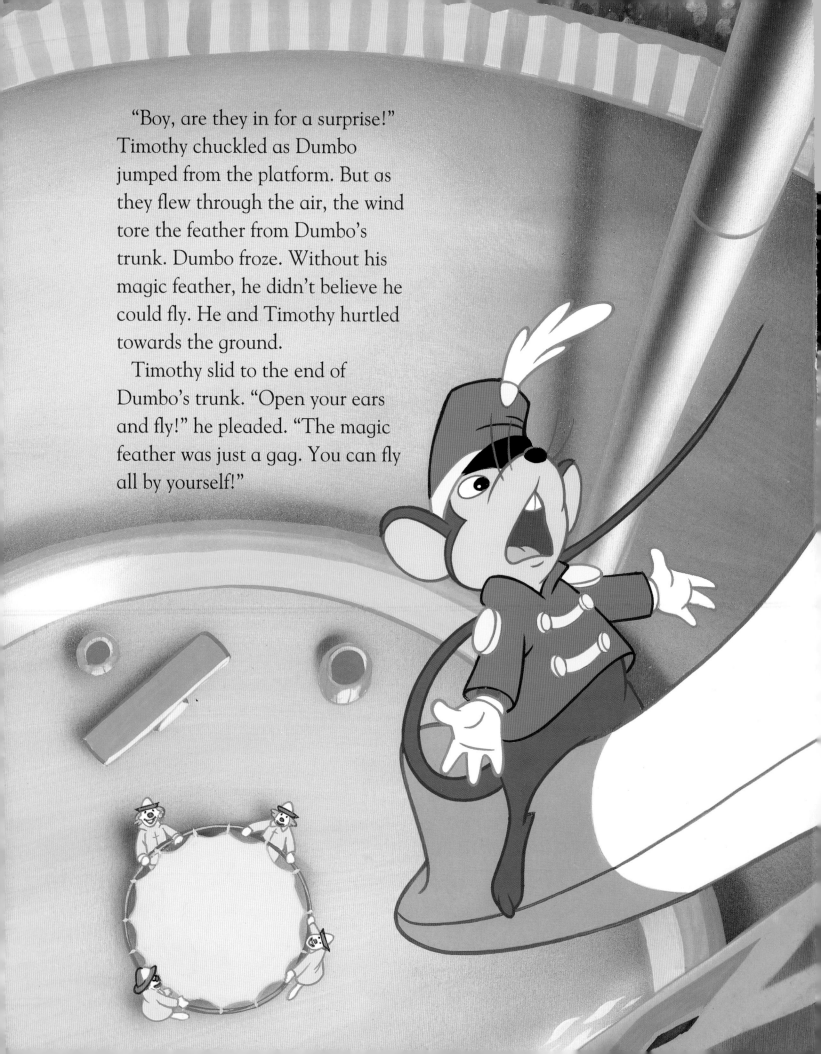

"Boy, are they in for a surprise!" Timothy chuckled as Dumbo jumped from the platform. But as they flew through the air, the wind tore the feather from Dumbo's trunk. Dumbo froze. Without his magic feather, he didn't believe he could fly. He and Timothy hurtled towards the ground.

Timothy slid to the end of Dumbo's trunk. "Open your ears and fly!" he pleaded. "The magic feather was just a gag. You can fly all by yourself!"

Dumbo heard Timothy's words and believed them. And what's more, he believed in himself. At the last second, Dumbo spread his ears, soaring up and up and up.

The astonished audience went wild as Dumbo zoomed after the clowns, chasing them around the ring. The crowd roared as he dove at the Ringmaster. They applauded thunderously as Dumbo did loop-the-loops and rolls and spins in the air.

Dumbo was famous. All the newspapers carried pictures of him and Timothy. Most importantly, Mrs Jumbo was let out of the carriage where she was being held, because the Ringmaster was so pleased with Dumbo. Dumbo thought it was great fun being a star. But what he loved best of all ... was being with his mother once again.